**Also b**  D0103801

Danger Guys Blast Off

## Coming Soon:

Danger Guys: Hollywood Halloween

# DANGER GUYS

## by Tony Abbott
## illustrated by Joanne Scribner

HarperTrophy
*A Division of* HarperCollins*Publishers*

Danger Guys
Text copyright © 1994 by Robert Abbott
Illustrations copyright © 1994 by Joanne L. Scribner

Library of Congress Cataloging-in-Publication Data
Abbott, Tony.
    Danger Guys / by Tony Abbott ; illustrated by Joanne Scribner.
        p.      cm.
    Summary: While attending the grand opening of Danger Guy, an adven-
ture store, Noodle and Zeek become involved with thieves who are loot-
ing an ancient temple and stealing its artifacts.
    ISBN 0-06-440519-2 (pbk.)
    [1. Adventure and adventurers—Fiction.]    I. Scribner, Joanne, ill.
II. Title.
PZ7.A1587Dan    1994                                      93-29799
[Fic]—dc20                                                    CIP
                                                              AC

Typography by Stefanie Rosenfeld
2   3   4   5   6   7   8   9   10
❖
First Harper Trophy Edition

**For Dolores, with love,
for so many reasons**

# ONE

It was a Saturday morning. I was dreaming of hot, buttery waffles.

I always dream of waffles in the morning.

The butter was just beginning to melt.

I was reaching for the syrup.

All of a sudden—*bang!*—my window flew open. My best friend, Zeek Pilinsky, came tumbling in.

"Danger!" he screamed.

"Where? Here?" I yelled. I fell out of bed.

"No, Noodle. At the Mayville Mall. The new adventure store, Danger Guy, opens today! Leather jackets. Army belts. Adventure stuff!"

Zeek and I are crazy about adventure stuff.

We've seen every action movie ever made. We've read every book.

We make a great team.

Zeek is the softball star in my class. He's the one with the muscles.

I'm the smart guy who thinks up the plans.

That's why Zeek calls me Noodle.

Now everybody calls me Noodle. Well, everybody except my mom. She calls me—

"Henry Newton! I won't say this again. Your breakfast is ready!"

Yep, that was my mom, calling up from the kitchen.

Boy, was she surprised when I told her to put a hold on the waffles. "This is business, Mom. But don't worry," I said, "we'll be back for lunch."

I gave her the thumbs-up sign. That meant everything was a-okay.

———

We ran the whole way to the mall. We made it there in under five minutes.

"Hurry," Zeek said, huffing.

"Hurry?" I said. "We got here in record time. What's the rush?"

Zeek gave me a look. "The first ten people in the store get FREE STUFF! Remember?"

I whizzed past him. "I think it's just around the corner," I said.

Then we saw it. On one side was a place called the Grandma Shop. It sold shoes and hats and lipsticks. On the other side was an underwear store.

Straight ahead was . . . a jungle!

"Holy cow!" I cried.

Big, crazy plants were growing out of the front of the store. There was an old leather satchel slung over a high branch. Rolled-up maps and charts were sticking out of it.

Next to that a beat-up wooden sign was nailed to a fake tree. DANGER GUY, it said in cracked letters. An arrow pointed

to a narrow winding path through the jungle.

"Perfect!" Zeek gasped. He slapped my arm and smiled. "This is the real thing, buddy."

I looked ahead through the leaves. The owner of the store was handing out prize tickets to the first ten people. I heard him say that the drawing, to find out who won what prize, would be in one hour. You had to be there to win.

No problem, I thought. We'd be there for a long time. I counted the heads in front of me. There were only eight.

"We made it!" I shouted.

Then, just as I was pushing the leaves aside to go in, I heard a funny sound behind me. It went something like "Umph!"

I whirled around. Zeek was falling over backward, grabbing at the bushes.

"Hey, Zeekie." I laughed. "That's not the way into the store."

But the next thing I knew I was face-to-face with two very big guys.

Boy, were they huge. Their pants and shirts were dirty. Their shoes were all caked with mud. And they had looks on their faces that I'd rather forget.

They had pushed Zeek aside. Now they were coming toward me. They wanted something. They wanted it bad. And I was in the way.

"Umph!"

Yep, I was in the bushes, too.

John Scribner

# TWO

**H**ey!" I shouted as I tumbled through the branches. "How rude can you get? You stole our places. Those prize tickets belong to us. We want our tickets!"

The men stopped and turned. One of them came over to me.

"Oops, " I said. "Did I say that?"

The guy put his huge face right up to mine. His cheeks were red and puffy. He was breathing so hard it made his mustache quiver.

Great. Now I'll *never* forget that face.

"Kid," he said, "we don't want your *dumb* prizes!" Then he took the tickets and pressed them right on my forehead.

They stuck there.

Before I could say thanks, he turned and disappeared into the store with his friend.

Zeek scrambled up from the floor and gave me a hand.

"Whew, that was weird," he said, dusting me off. "Definitely a guy with an attitude."

"Yeah, and what a face! I don't mind if I never see him again."

"What's the deal with those guys, anyway, Noodle? I mean, who do they think they are, pushing us around?"

I shrugged. "I don't know, yet. But maybe we'll find out, if we keep our eyes and ears open. They're still here somewhere. Let's keep a lookout for them."

Then Zeek glanced up at my forehead and laughed. "Neat trick," he said, pointing to the tickets.

"Yeah," I told him, "it comes in handy." I peeled the tickets off and gave him one.

"Now come on. We have some serious exploring to do before they announce the prizes."

Zeek pushed his ticket into his pocket and nodded. I smiled and gave him the thumbs-up sign.

He gave me one, too.

Danger Guy was even better than we expected. It was crammed with terrific adventure gear.

The whole front of the store was set up like a jungle outpost. Tents and canteens. Flashlights and climbing ropes. Binoculars and boots.

On one side was a field table with a stack of ancient maps, a compass, and an old radio.

"Wow!" I said to Zeek. "Does it get any better than this?"

On the wall was an old, cracked photo of Dr. Livingstone, the famous explorer of Africa.

Next to him was a picture of Indiana Jones. "Great hat," I said. Zeek grinned at me.

At the end was a shot of the Emersons, the famous husband-and-wife exploring team. I had read all about their adventures. They explored old ruins and wrote books about them.

Mr. Emerson had a beard. Mrs. Emerson wore glasses and her hair was all bunched up in the back. She looked like a teacher.

They were standing in a jungle, next to a truck full of exploring gear. Both of them were smiling.

"Yeah," said Zeek. "I'd be smiling too if I had equipment like that."

I was turning around to look at the supply belts when someone bumped into me. Hey, I thought, this is getting to be a habit.

It was the big guy's friend, the quiet one. He was carrying a dirty wooden crate.

He took it to the front of the store. He

set it down, opened it, and began putting incredible stuff out on some empty shelves.

Golden masks. Little statues. Jewelry. Things like that.

"Hey." I nudged Zeek. "Ancient artifacts! I wonder where they get this stuff."

"Never mind that," he said. "Look over your shoulder."

Behind me, the big guy with the mustache was having some kind of argument with the store owner.

He kept poking his finger at the owner and growling at him. I couldn't hear more than a few words of what he was saying.

"Truck . . . dig . . . money . . . or else!"

Finally the owner just nodded his head, slowly. Whatever it was, it seemed like he'd just lost the argument.

"Zeek," I whispered. "I don't like what's going on here."

But Zeek was in the back of the store waving to me. "Noodle, get over here. The

best stuff is this way."

I followed him.

That's when everything really started to happen.

We headed back through a doorway into a small room. It was piled high with cartons and crates like those they had everywhere else in the store. Except that a lot of them were nailed shut. And some of them were caked with dirt.

"This room isn't part of the store," I said to Zeek.

"Naah," he said. "This is Danger Guy. It's all part of the adventure."

"Um . . . I don't know," I said. "Something just doesn't feel right."

But before I could say another word— *ka-thunk!*—the door slammed shut behind us. Suddenly it was dark.

Then a motor started. It was loud. Like a truck motor. Zeek grabbed my arm.

The floor jerked under us and we began to move.

"Hey!" we yelled. "We're in here!"

It was too late.

Within seconds a truck with Zeek and me in the back of it was screeching away from the store. Away from the mall. And away from Mayville, too.

# THREE

**W**hoa!" I said. "Stop! Get us out of here!"

Silly me. It was way too late for that. Zeek and I were trapped.

"W-w-what happened?" Zeek said. His voice came from somewhere on the floor.

"Well, pal, it's like I said. This room isn't part of the store."

I could sense him giving me a look. "Lucky guess," he said.

"Okay," I said. "So it's dark. So we're trapped in a truck. But, hey, we can handle this. We're professionals, right?"

The truck was speeding along smoothly. It seemed as if we were on a highway.

"We're doomed," said Zeek.

"No way. Well, not yet, at least," I said, trying to cheer him up. "Rule number one, Zeek—get to know your surroundings."

I felt around for a flashlight. I found one and flicked it on. We took a closer look at the boxes of equipment.

"Look at this stuff," I said. "Heavy-duty. Picks, axes, shovels. Army flashlights. Packs. Jackets. Belts. This is real adventure gear. Some of it must be stolen from the store. And I bet it has something to do with those two guys."

Zeek nodded. "You mean Mr. Big might be up there behind the wheel right now? Oh, great!"

"Listen, Zeek," I said. "I don't know what's going to happen next. But maybe we should be ready for whatever it is."

I grabbed a backpack and tossed him another. "You know what I mean?"

He got the idea right away.

"Yeah, let's suit up!"

We pulled on a couple of leather jackets. We jammed our packs with everything we could find. Flashlights, supply belts, workshirts, hats, climbing ropes, goggles—the works.

There were even some mess kits with gray-looking food junk inside. We packed some just in case.

Okay. We looked terrific. We were ready.

Just then the truck made a sharp turn.

"Whoa! We're leaving the highway," I whispered. "And we're going uphill. If only we could get a look outside."

Zeek held up his hand. "Wait. I think we're changing course again."

Suddenly the truck drove into a rut and jolted back up in the air. *Ping! Clunk!*

I smelled something. A whiff of cool, wet air shot in. It came from . . . outside!

That's it! The back door of the truck had just jerked open.

Zeek and I both stared out. We expected to see houses, trees, roads—something!

But we couldn't see a thing. It was dark outside.

"Wait a minute," I said. "It was morning when we got trapped in here. And we haven't been traveling that long. Maybe . . ."

Zeek and I jumped up at the same time.

"We're underground!"

Zeek crawled over to the door. "Maybe I can see something."

"Careful," I whispered.

The truck started making some sharp turns. It swerved a few times to the right, then to the left. I tried to figure out how many turns the truck made. Just in case we needed to backtrack. But I lost count.

Then there must have been something in the road because the truck bounced suddenly.

*Wham!* I went flying. In fact, everything in the truck jumped and then landed with a crash.

I found myself stuck between a crate of snorkels and a carton of weather balloons. I grabbed a few of each.

"Well, Zeek, what do you see? Can you make out anything?"

He didn't answer.

"Hey, Zeek? Are you okay?"

No answer.

I whirled the flashlight around the inside of the truck. Crates, boxes, jackets, shovels, me.

Yeah, everything was there, all right.

Everything but Zeek.

# FOUR

**Z**EEKIE!"

No Zeekie.

I was alone in the truck.

Terrific. I've lost Zeek. His parents will kill me.

I had to think fast. I still couldn't see a thing. I still didn't know where I was.

The only person I could count on in all this mess was Zeek. And he was out there somewhere.

There was only one thing to do.

I grabbed some extra gear. I tightened my pack. I took one last look around. And then I jumped.

———

If I had eaten waffles that morning I might have been a little softer. I might have bounced a few more times.

But I was lucky. The truck was slowing down when I hit the ground. When I finally rolled to a stop, I wasn't hurt.

I dusted myself off and flashed my light all around. I was in some kind of tunnel. An underground cave with jagged rocks on the sides.

I stamped my foot. Yeah, just as I thought. It splashed.

And there was that wet-rock smell again. I didn't know anything for sure yet. But things were starting to click in my head.

First things first. Find Zeek. If I could.

I headed back up the tunnel. Then I heard it.

"OOOAAAH!"

Oh, boy. So I wasn't alone after all. I grabbed a rock.

But right there, just a few steps away, was a face. A face without a body.

It was like a ghost's head. Just hanging there in the darkness. It was horrible.

And it was smiling.

"You rat!" I said. "I thought you really *were* a ghost."

Zeek pulled the flashlight away from his chin.

"Sorry, buddy. I thought it might be one of the big guys. And I wanted to scare him before he scared me. Are you okay?"

Yeah, it felt good to be together again.

"I'm just terrific. Now let's stick close, all right?"

"Sure." Zeek shined his flashlight down the tunnel ahead of us. "But which way do we go? I mean, I lost my way five times just looking for you. There are a lot of caves leading off from this one. How do we know which one heads out?"

"I've been thinking about that," I said. "We should be able to find the way by following the heat."

"By following what?"

"The heat. Listen, it's a hot day out

there, right? Well, it's always cooler the deeper underground you are. We'll know we're getting to the entrance when the air feels warmer."

Zeek was quiet for a minute. "But isn't the center of the earth hot, too? You know, like hell?"

I didn't answer him. I looked both ways and then chose a direction. "Come on. And don't wander off. Just do what I do."

"But one thing I found out," said Zeek, "there are a lot of potholes. Don't fall into one."

Too late. With my next step my foot slipped on something. The ground gave way under me.

"Help!"

But Zeek couldn't help me now. I was slipping down, right in front of his face.

Before I knew it—*zoom!*—I was flat on my back, shooting down an underground passage like a human rocket.

Everything was a blur.

My feet were skidding along in front of me.

My pants were getting pushed up to my knees. I was starting to feel sick.

Then something hit my shoulder. It was a shoe. There was a foot in it.

"Zeek!"

"You said stick together. But this is too much! Can't you stop us?"

I dug my feet in. I held out my arms. But we didn't stop. We didn't even slow down.

"No way! The tunnel is getting steeper. We're really starting to pick up speed now."

We rolled through some crazy loops. We dived into hairpin turns and shot back out again. My rear was beginning to feel like mush.

And just when I thought the ride couldn't get any faster, the tunnel got wet. Very wet.

Now we *really* took off.

"Water slide!" I yelled.

Zeek sputtered behind me, "Oh, no! Like that crazy one near my house!"

I thought of that superfast, superscary water slide. It had a funny name . . .

Then—*whoosh!*—we took a high turn and bounced.

When we came down, there was no more slide. No more rocks. No more anything. We were flying through the air.

Then I remembered the name of the water slide. I wished I hadn't.

"Instant Death!" I screamed as we stopped flying and started to fall.

# FIVE

**W**e just had time to pinch our noses before . . .

*Splish!* That was me.

*Splash!* That was Zeek.

We came down hard. Lucky for us, the pool we landed in wasn't too shallow. Unlucky for us, it wasn't a pool but a river. As soon as we hit the water, it started to pull us along.

But that wasn't all. I could hear something up ahead. "Hey, what's that rumbling noise?"

"What else?" yelled Zeek. "Rapids. A waterfall. A hundred man-eating sharks. I'll let you know when I get there."

Yeah, Zeek was being funny. But he was drifting fast. And when I bobbed up to see, I saw that he was right. Just ahead of him were the whitecaps of a swirling rapids.

"Hold on, buddy, I'm coming." I reached for my rope, made a quick loop, and threw it toward the bank. It snagged on a rock.

"Zeek, grab my hand," I yelled.

"I can't reach it!" he said. He was really starting to splash around.

The only thing to do was to let myself float closer to him. Right away I felt the pull of the current, but I held my arm out as far as I could.

Finally he splashed over and caught my hand. After a lot of pulling on the rope, we made it to the bank.

We just sat there, trying to catch our breaths. Zeek was shaking his head. "Man, I hate getting wet!"

After a couple of minutes he turned to me. "By the way, thanks, pal. I was almost a goner."

"Hey," I said. "All part of the job. But

come on, let's see if we can get out of here."

I flicked on my flashlight and stood it up on the ground. We were on a narrow path along the bank. A lot of side tunnels led away and into the mountain.

"Well, one thing's for sure," I said, looking up at the ceiling that we had just dropped through. "We can't go back the way we came."

"Right. Unless you know how to go *up* a water slide." Zeek smiled as he squeezed out his socks. "But where are we, anyway?"

I pulled a compass from my backpack. I shook it dry and held it to the flashlight. "Well, we're nowhere near Mayville . . . and . . ."

Zeek blinked at me. "And?"

"And judging by the time it took to get here, we must be somewhere in the Maderos Mountains."

Zeek started shaking his head again. "Noodle, we're doomed for sure. We'll die

in this cave, and fifty years from now they'll find our skeletons with our backpacks on them!"

It hit me, too. Here we were, at least fifty miles from home, way underground, with no idea of how to get out.

I thought of my mom and dad. I thought of school and of my whole life ahead of me.

I thought of the waffles I never had that morning.

"Hey, I'm hungry," I cried.

Zeek tossed me his mess kit with that crusty gray food junk inside.

"Thanks," I said. "You just cured my hunger."

"Shh!" said Zeek. "And kill the light."

I switched off my flashlight. There was a faint glimmer coming from one of the side tunnels.

"Daylight!" I cried. "We're saved!"

Zeek held up his hand. "I don't think so, Noodle."

Voices were coming from the tunnel. They didn't sound friendly. They were yelling pretty loudly about something. And one voice was shouting louder than the others.

"Uh-oh," I whispered. "Mr. Big. I knew we'd meet up with him again. And it sounds like he's still got his attitude."

I remembered that face and shivered.

"He's got friends, too," Zeek said, creeping a little closer. "What if they catch us and think we're spying on them?"

I thought about it. "Well, we can stay here until the gray food turns black. Or we can try to get out."

"Yeah, but who knows what they'll do to us?"

"First of all," I said, "maybe they won't see us. But if they do, we don't know anything, do we? So we'll tell them it's all a mistake. No problem."

But when we peeked into the tunnel, we saw that it *was* a problem.

# SIX

We were looking into an enormous cave. It was bright, but not with daylight. A searchlight beamed over on one side. Lots of mean-looking guys were hustling around everywhere.

I nudged Zeek and pointed. "Look. It's Mr. Big, all right." There was no mistake. That mustache. That mean look.

He must have driven the truck here. And now he was staring into the back of it and slamming his fist against the door.

"I guess he just noticed the stuff we took," Zeek whispered.

"Too bad," I said, thinking about the way he had pushed the tickets onto my forehead. "He should have thought of that before he locked us in."

That's when I saw it.

At the far end of the cave, sticking out of the rocks, was a huge stone doorway. The sides of it were decorated with gold and shiny gems.

I could see that two enormous stones had been moved aside and the opening led deep into the mountain.

"An ancient temple!"

"Holy cow," Zeek whispered. "Is that what these guys are after?"

I pulled out my binoculars to get a better look. Giant pictures were carved into the rock. Weird men with wings and lots of heads. Tigers with ten legs and bird beaks.

And all of them were covered with jewels and golden ornaments.

"Zeek, this isn't any fake storefront. This is the real thing."

The men were busy working around the giant doorway. Some had wheelbarrows. Some had picks and shovels. They were digging in the temple and loading crates with the stuff they were finding.

"Treasure thieves," I said. "It doesn't look good."

And what I saw next didn't look good, either. Up on a ledge a man and a woman were sitting on the ground. They looked familiar. The man had a beard. The woman wore glasses. Both of them were tied up with thick rope.

"The Emersons!" I gasped. "It's the husband-and-wife exploring team. Their picture is on the wall of the store."

Zeek looked at me. "Noodle, this is the real thing, all right. Those people need our help."

I knew he was right. We couldn't just walk away, even if we did know the way out. Which we didn't. "Yeah, Zeek, if we ever had to be Danger Guys, now is the time. Are you ready?"

He gave me a thumbs-up.

I smiled. Ditto.

So we crawled into the cave quietly. We

were careful to stay in the shadows. Some rocks up ahead gave us pretty good cover. We rolled behind them and poked our heads up.

When no one was looking, Zeek tossed a rope up to the ledge. It looped around a rock and dangled in the shadows. Slowly we climbed up the face of the rock.

I was the first one over the top.

When the Emersons saw me, they almost fell over. I guess they weren't expecting anybody to rescue them.

I put my finger to my lips, and Zeek and I untied them without a sound. Then I pointed behind some rocks. They got the idea right away.

"I can't believe it," Mrs. Emerson said when she was free. "Where did you two kids come from?"

We told them who we were and how we'd gotten there. They were pretty happy to see us.

"My wife and I are writing a book about this ancient temple, " Mr. Emerson said.

"But yesterday those men came with trucks. They tied us up and started digging."

Suddenly, everything fell into place.

"I've got it! " I said. "These guys are stealing treasures from the temple and selling them at the Mayville Mall. Mr. Big and his friend were delivering the stuff to Danger Guy this morning. They probably figured that an adventure store would make a perfect cover."

"That must be right," said Mrs. Emerson. "I guess they don't call you Noodle for nothing!"

"Thanks. " I smiled. "Now come on, let's get out of here before these guys spot us."

I slung the rope over my shoulder and started back down the ledge.

"Noodle, you're wet," Mrs. Emerson said. I guess she had just noticed the puddles I was making as I walked.

"A little," I said. "We got dunked in the river that's down that tunnel."

"Yeah, me, too," said Zeek. "No thanks

to Noodle. But don't worry, we're drying off."

Mrs. Emerson turned to her husband. "It's worse than we thought," she said.

Mr. Emerson didn't seem happy. In fact, he suddenly turned a little gray, like that food junk. "Boys, I'm afraid we'll never make it out of this cave alive. The whole temple is going to explode."

I stopped. I glanced back at Zeek. He looked kind of sick. I guess I looked the same.

"Did you say 'explode'? You mean like . . . *Ka-boom*?"

"That's right," Mr. Emerson said. "And from what you just told us, I'd say we have less than ten minutes!"

# SEVEN

Zeek slumped down on the ground. "I knew it," he groaned. "We really *are* doomed."

I looked at Mr. Emerson. I thought he would smile and say it was all a joke. But he didn't.

"You see, boys, this temple was built under a huge underground lake. And the ancient people who built it booby-trapped it against treasure thieves."

"Booby-trapped it? How?" I asked, shooting a look over at Zeek. He just sat there, staring at his watch. "Ten minutes," he muttered.

"If the great door of the temple is ever forced open," Mrs. Emerson went on, "then the lake above us starts to drain. A little at first. Then a lot."

"I get it. The river Zeek and I fell into was the lake draining."

"Right. And when the water reaches a certain level, the front of the temple will burst open, just like a dam breaking. The whole cave will be flooded."

"But there must be a quick way out of here," I asked. "Isn't there?"

I was hoping they'd say "Sure! Right this way!"

"No" was all they said.

"Nine minutes," Zeek said.

"Okay, okay," I said. "Plan B. Is there any way to stop the flooding?"

The Emersons looked at each other.

"Well," said Mr. Emerson, "there is a hidden room near the top of the temple. It's supposed to be where the most precious artifacts are hidden. The legend says that if you can get there and find something called the Eye of the Sun, then the flooding is supposed to stop."

Just then we heard something pop in the cave.

"Look!" Zeek gasped. He was pointing to a thin stream of water trickling down the temple wall. "I guess it's already started."

"Okay," I said. "We'll do it, whatever it is. Where is this secret room, anyway?"

"No one knows, exactly. But we think it should be somewhere over there." Mrs. Emerson motioned to where the water was fizzling out of the stones.

I looked around. A ledge led away from where we were. It was really narrow, only about a foot wide, and about a hundred feet up from the cave floor. It was just wide enough for a couple of kids. The Emersons would never make it.

Zeek stood up and slapped me on the

back. "It looks like we go rock climbing, buddy."

I tightened my gear. "You folks stay here," I said to the Emersons. "Zeek and I will do what we can."

# EIGHT

I gulped hard as we started along the ledge. Lucky me, I got to go first.

My nose was pressed against the rocks. My hands were groping for something, anything, to hold on to. My feet were inching along a narrow strip of rock trying not to fall to an instant death.

And Zeek was right behind me, pushing and nudging me with every step.

"Not so close!" I huffed. "I can't exactly skip along, you know."

"Eight minutes," he gasped. That was all he said. I got the point and hustled along.

A couple of minutes later we were near

the top of the temple when my foot slipped on some loose rocks. Suddenly, Mr. Big shot around and looked straight up at us.

"Everybody shut up!" he screamed. The digging stopped; the cave went silent. Then he pointed and yelled, "Searchlight! Let's see what's up there!"

I didn't have time to think—my body took over. "Dive!" I gasped.

We dived into the shadows, but where I expected to feel solid rock, there was nothing.

Oh, no, a bottomless pit!

But it wasn't. We tumbled down into a small cave. At least I thought it was a cave. I couldn't see because there was a blinding light in my eyes.

"Noodle! The searchlight!"

I squinted and looked around. "Huh-uh, Zeek, it's not the searchlight."

There was a hole in the ceiling, a shaft that went up a long way and ended with a bright light. "It's . . . daylight! It's the great outdoors! Hooray! We're home. It's just up there!"

Zeek squinted up at the shaft. "Just up there? Just a *hundred feet* up there! We'll never make it, Nood. Besides, I think I hear Mr. Big coming. And we've still got to find the secret room, remember?"

"Wait a second, Zeek."

My eyes had just gotten used to the bright light. What I saw made everything go quiet in my head.

All around the walls were gold masks and statues of mysterious creatures. Old leather sacks filled with necklaces and jewels and golden ornaments were piled high everywhere.

And in the center of it all, just under the shaft of light, was a huge golden ball. It must have been ten feet high. A round red circle was painted on the side.

"The Eye of the Sun!" I cried. "Zeek, this is it! We're in the secret room!"

"All right!" cried Zeek, punching the air. Then he frowned. "But now what? I mean, how are we supposed to stop the flooding with this?"

"I'm thinking, I'm thinking." Then something caught my eye. There was a groove cut into the floor. It led away from the stone and down a side tunnel into the darkness.

"How's this?" I said. "Maybe if we move the ball, it rolls down the tunnel and plugs up some kind of drain hole at the other end."

Zeek gave me one of his looks. "Come on, Noodle. How could we possibly move it? It must weigh a ton and it's been here for a couple hundred years. "

I laughed. "It weighs *ten* tons at least and it's been here for a *thousand* years. But have you got a better idea?"

He looked around the secret room, then looked at his watch. "Nope. Sounds great!"

"Okay then. We both push at the same time. Ready? ONE!"

We heaved until our faces turned blue.

Nothing. The stone hadn't budged an inch.

We dug our feet in.

"TWO!"

Some dust slid off the top of the Eye.

"Okay, this time we give it all we have."

"THREE!"

Suddenly, the Eye of the Sun shifted on the floor. It teetered and wobbled and finally—*vrrrrooommm*—started to roll down the groove.

"We did it!"

We did it, all right. We backed up while the Eye rolled across the floor. We watched it slowly pick up speed. We saw it heading for the tunnel. But we forgot to get out of the way.

# NINE

*V*rrrooommm!

In seconds we were running for our lives. The Eye of the Sun was barreling down behind us like a speeding train.

"NooOOooOOoodle! We're doomed!" Zeek's yell echoed through the dark passage. I wondered if he was finally right.

If we fell, the stone would crush us. But how long could we keep on running flat-out?

"Noodle," Zeek gasped out. "I know what we're running from. But what are we running *to*?"

He didn't have to wait long for an answer. If anything was louder than the roar of that oversized bowling ball behind us, it was the swirling, churning, gurgling noise up ahead.

"Whirlpool!" I yelped. We were running straight for the lake's huge drain. It would suck us down in a second. I had to think fast.

"Zeek, stick your arms out and reach for the wall. If you feel any kind of space, dive for it! We have to let the rock slide past us or we're doomed."

An instant later I felt a rough hollow on the side of the tunnel next to me. I jumped for it and went flat against the wall.

*Vrooom!* The Eye rumbled past me.

"Zeekie!" I yelled. But all I could hear was the stone grinding down the tunnel and the deafening roar at the end of it.

Suddenly, there was a huge crash as the Eye of the Sun jumped out of the tunnel and hit the water.

It must have gone straight to the bottom and plugged the hole. In a few seconds the lake stopped churning, the rumbling stopped, and the tunnel was silent.

"Zeek!" I cried again. The word echoed around and around in the quiet.

Then there he was. Just like his old self.

"That stupid eyeball chased me all the way down to the lake. Luckily I had these." He held up a face mask and a snorkel. "Boy, I hate getting wet. And just when I was starting to dry out, too."

"Okay, pal," I said. "You deserve a break." We started back up the tunnel.

But when we entered the secret room, the Emersons were waiting for us.

"Good work, boys!" said Mr. Emerson. "But our troubles aren't over. The thieves have discovered that we're gone. They're coming up the ledge right now."

We could hear the voices coming closer.

"Noodle! Think of something. Anything."

"Don't worry, I'll figure something out," I said, bluffing. "But even if we do get

away, we won't get far on foot. This mountain is miles from the nearest town. If there was a radio, we could call for help."

"There *is* a radio," Mrs. Emerson said. "But it's over there." She moved over to the ledge and pointed down into the cave.

There was a radio, all right. It was sitting on an old dusty crate by the temple entrance, surrounded by a bunch of thieves.

"We'll never get to it." Mrs. Emerson sighed.

I looked around the cave. Zeek did, too. We started to smile at each other. We were thinking the same thing.

"I think we have a plan," I said.

"Is it dangerous?" asked Mr. Emerson.

We smiled again. "You bet!"

Suddenly, there was a noise. It sounded like a growl.

"Oh, no, they've got dogs!" Zeek gasped.

# TEN

There it was again. *Grrr!*

It was close. *Grrr-rrr!*

It was *real* close.

It was my stomach. It wanted waffles.

Everybody laughed.

"Okay, okay," I said. "Mr. Big's on our tail and we've got a job to do. Here's the plan."

I dug into my backpack and began handing out supplies. Zeek did the same.

I gave Mr. Emerson some weather balloons. I told him to fill them and then put some of the extra shirts and hats on them.

I handed Mrs. Emerson a couple of

flashlights. "When I go, you start waving these around."

"Where are you going?" Mrs. Emerson asked.

"You'll see!"

Next I tied a loop in my rope and with Zeek's help flung it out across the cave. It circled around the head of a stone statue. The statue had a bird's head and four arms.

Zeek picked up a stick and a rock. "Ready?" he asked.

I turned to the Emersons. "Now you'll see what Zeek is famous for."

I glanced around. Everything looked perfect. "Ready!" I shouted.

Zeek tossed the rock up and batted it hard. Home run! It whizzed across the cave.

Crash! The searchlight went dark. Mr. Big and his friends started yelling.

"Now it's my turn," I said. And I jumped off the ledge, holding the rope.

"Daaanggerrr Guuuyyy!" I hollered. My

voice echoed through the cave. It was great!

Zeek batted rocks all around the walls, at the truck, and at Mr. Big and his friends. The thieves were going crazy.

Mr. Big slipped off the ledge and rolled back down to the cave floor. His friends didn't know what was going on.

Then Mr. Emerson let the balloons go.

They floated all around the cave. When Mrs. Emerson waved the flashlights it looked like there were hundreds of us!

The treasure thieves got scared and started to run into one another. They thought they were under attack.

And all the time I was swinging through the air yelling my head off! Does it get any better?

# ELEVEN

In a flash I was back on the ledge with the radio in my arms.

Mr. Emerson quickly called the police.

But there was still the problem of getting out of there. It wouldn't be long before Mr. Big figured out that there were only four of us. And we were way outnumbered.

"Come on, Noodle, tell us your plan!" Zeek was jumping up and down. "If you don't come up with something, we're really doomed!"

Then it hit me. Yeah, okay, it's just crazy enough to work. I looked at Zeek. He looked scared. But I punched my thumb in the air and that old smile started to come back. "Hey, buddy," I said, "would I let you down?"

"Hooray, we're saved!" Zeek was laughing now.

"It's a long shot," I admitted. "But it's really simple." I dug into my pack and pulled out some more weather balloons. "Here, just hold on tight and let's go."

Zeek's face fell. "Go? Go where?"

I pointed to the light shaft above us. "There! It goes all the way up to the surface. Easy. You just flip this tab . . ."

I pulled a little tab on the bottom of the balloon and held on tight as it started to inflate.

A couple of seconds later my feet left the ground and I started to float up toward the shaft.

"Come on, Danger Guy. Try it!" I reached over and flipped Zeek's tab, too.

"Noodle? Noodle! Whoa!"

When we got to the top, we tossed our

ropes down. The Emersons climbed up after us.

It didn't take long for the police to get there. A helicopter rescued us from the top of the mountain. Then we watched while a team of state troopers stormed the cave and rounded up the treasure thieves.

Poor Mr. Big! He came out of the cave with handcuffs on. He was growling to himself, and he had a strange look in his eyes. He still didn't know what had hit him.

Then Zeek turned to me and frowned. "But does that mean that the Danger Guy store is part of all this?"

"I don't think so," I said. "The way Mr. Big was pushing the owner around this morning, I'd say he was forcing him to go along with the scheme."

Zeek smiled. "Great, because I want to see if they'll give me some free stuff for this ticket." He held up a soggy, chewed-up piece of paper.

I showed him mine—what was left of it.

"Hey, they don't call us Danger Guys for nothing!"

Zeek gave me the thumbs-up, and we both started to laugh. Yeah, we make a great team, all right. Does it get any better?

Well, our moms and dads were sure glad to see us. It was late at night, but my mom made me waffles anyway. She had to. My stomach was growling too loudly to talk!

At school Zeek and I were heroes. The town newspaper printed a story about us. The mayor declared a Noodle and Zeek Day. And Mr. and Mrs. Emerson dedicated their book to us.

Even though we weren't there for the prize drawing, it worked out okay. The owner of the store was so happy that Mr. Big and his gang had been caught, he said we could keep all the gear we had used in the rescue.

Leather jackets, hats, ropes, back-packs—everything!

But the best part of all happened today. We went to the mall. And there, on the wall of Danger Guy, was a new picture.

You guessed it. Zeek and me, next to all of the other adventure hounds.

Nope. It just doesn't get any better.

**Don't miss the next
dangerous adventure:**

# DANGER GUYS
## Blast Off

🚀 The Mayville carnival comes to town,
   and Noodle and Zeek are off for a
   day of fun.

🚀 All of a sudden their rocket ride
   goes haywire—the rocket is *real* and
   it's heading skyward!

🚀 The rocket's emergency crash
   landing brings Noodle and Zeek
   face to face with evil Dr. Morbius,
   a.k.a. Mr. Vazny, science teacher.

🚀 Our heroes must think fast . . .
   Dr. Morbius has a fiendish plot to
   blow up Mayville School, and only the
   Danger Guys can stop him!